PILATE
Robert A. Revel

PHAEDRUS PUBLISHING
Healdsburg, CA

PHAEDRUS PUBLISHING
128 Powell Ave., Healdsburg CA 95448
Design by Caren Parnes, Enterprising Graphics

ISBN-13: 978-0-692-27525-2
Library of Congress Control Number: 2014951319
® WGA Registration Number: 1717503

Printed in the United States of America

This play is dedicated to Robert Shannon Leannarda.

"Hey brother, you got another song left in you?"

CHARACTERS

in order of appearance

Zarah, *17 year-old Jewess. Pilate's forced mistress.*
Pontius Pilate, *Roman Prefect*
Staff Guard
Pharisee 1
Sentinel 1
Sentinel 2
Counsel Elder 2
Counsel Elder 3
Counsel Elder 4
Joseph Caiaphas, *Pharisee and Temple High Priest*
Secretary Septimus, *Pilate's secretary*
Lead Legionnaire
Jesus Christ, *Young Jewish Sage*
Palace Guard 1
Claudia, *Pilate's Wife*
"Crowd"
Captain
Posted Guard 1
Posted Guard 2
Vocal Priest
Conspiring Priest 1
Conspiring Priest 2
Conspiring Priest 3
Prison Guard
Single Centurion
Judas Iscariot, *Disciple of Jesus*
Roman Guard
Barrabas, *Convicted Jewish rebel*
Night Guard, *Father of sick child*
Guard 2
Centurion Captain
Execution Centurion 1
Execution Centurion 2
Execution Centurion 3
Execution Centurion 4

ACT I

EXT. DARK AND EMPTY STONE STREET - EVENING

Zarah, an exotically beautiful and striking 17-year-old Jewish female runs from the darkness of stage right and stops under a shaft of light. She is out of breath, clutching a wrap, looking ravaged and desperate. She speaks out toward the audience.

ZARAH: Between two worlds do I move. To neither do I belong. I occupy two beds, where my body lies in a state that knows nothing of the sweet sleep of the innocent. Orphans and feral cats have more station and belonging than does the soul that occupies this trampled garden.

She clutches her wrap again tightly and runs off into the darkness of stage left, away from where she came from.

INT. PREFECT PILATE'S PRAETORIUM OFFICE - DAY

A commotion of shuffling feet and voices is heard echoing in the outer corridor of the Prefects office. Pilate looks up from his task, and addresses his staff guard.

PILATE: What is this?

The Staff Guard moves deliberately toward the door to investigate, and exits. Pilate resumes his task.

After a few moments the Staff Guard returns.

STAFF GUARD: Prefect, members of the Jewish council are petitioning that a warrant of arrest be issued for a zealot named Jesus who hails from Galilee.

Pilate reflects a moment.

PILATE: I recall this petition. I sent word that I would not enforce it to the Sanhedrin.

STAFF GUARD: Yes Prefect. Well they are back again to

1

request this man's seizure, as they have by their own judicial review convicted him of heresy.

Pilate rolls his eyes.

PILATE: Another Baptist in the wilderness? Have they not appealed to Herod? The man abides in Galilee. It is within his jurisdiction.

STAFF GUARD: This man Jesus has come to Jerusalem sir. He is here now in the city.

Pilate nods.

PILATE: Bring them in.

The guard leaves and momentarily returns with two sentinels who are escorting in five Pharisee Council elders.

STAFF GUARD: *(to the Pharisees)* You are in the presence of the honorable Prefect Pontius Pilate. Speak only when you are asked to by the Prefect.

PILATE: Gentlemen, the matter of this Jesus individual has been before me and I have concluded that there was no cause for his arrest under Roman law, based on the complaints you have levied. Is there something more you wish to add to the complaint that I am not aware of? Or have you simply come to harass my office?

PHARISEE 1: Prefect, this man Jesus claims to be King of the Jews. He says he talks to God! It is blasphemy and heresy under our law, punishable by death.

Pilate seems unimpressed with any Jewish penal code, and the Pharisee speaking can sense it.

PHARISEE 1: Prefect, if I may say, his claim of sovereignty over the Jewish people is not only false, it is treason and sedition before Roman law.

PILATE: I am touched over your genuine concern about the Republic of Rome. Perhaps even a bit entertained at your citation of Roman legal doctrine concerning treason and sedition. However, you fail to convince me that you are not attempting to use my office as some sort of mercenary power to seize an individual your council finds distasteful. Why buzz around my office over this Nazarene? Go. Entreat Herod to do your dirty work, as you did with the Baptist.

The Council priests look at one another uncomfortably.

PILATE: Do I need to mention that this kind of manipulative activity around my office, is in fact, the sort of nuisance that I will issue arrest warrants for?

The Chief Priest of the Sanhedrin Council, Caiaphas, steps forward to speak.

CAIAPHAS: Prefect, forgive our clumsy attempt at appealing to the better natures of your esteemed office. We have failed to make our concerns clear, and so we return to assure you that they are legitimate and hopefully worthy of your consideration.

Pilate nods at this note of reason, and gestures to the more tactful council elder.

PILATE: I have heard very little that is worthy of my consideration thus far.

CAIAPHAS: Prefect, this man, Jesus of Nazareth, is a menace to our people. He misrepresents our culture and our values. Many of our people in Galilee dangerously refer to him as Rabbi, though he holds no such title or authority. He communes with harlots and the untouchables. Now he comes to Jerusalem to mock our traditions and customs during Passover.

PILATE: So he is a Nazarene temple hater. This is no affair of Rome's.

CAIAPHAS: But Prefect, we observe lately, that not only does he desecrate the traditions we hold dear, he turns over the tables of the moneychangers in the temple in a rage. He converts even tax collectors into following him, and we fear he may one day soon, in the name of Judea, boldly assault or strike out against the Empire of Rome, claiming he is a Messiah of our people, as indeed his radical followers already believe he is. We do not want this man to be mistaken as representing the Jewish people when he finally lashes out against the Roman State. We fear a swift and misplaced reprisal against law abiding Jews may result from such a calamity, and we are here to prevent such a dangerous misunderstanding from occurring, particularly over Passover, as he moves now in the city.

The argument has merit and is well spoken to Pilate's ear.

PILATE: I will have him brought before me. I will assess if this man is a threat to anyone, and I alone will determine his fate. That will conclude the matter of this man, Jesus of Nazareth, and you will accept my judgment and never again approach my office regarding the matter for any reason. Is that clear, gentlemen?

All the Sanhedrin Council members nod in affirmation.

CAIAPHAS: Thank you, Prefect.

The group is escorted from the room.

PILATE: *(to his guard)* Arrest Jesus of Nazareth. Bring him before me, alive.

STAFF GUARD: Yes, Prefect.

INT. PILATE'S PRIVATE CHAMBER - NIGHT

Pilate sits alone near the balcony of his private chamber watching the last of the day's sun set beyond the horizon. He seems withdrawn and contemplative. He shows no emotion as he sits quietly.

After several moments Pilate's secretary Septimus enters.

SECRETARY SEPTIMUS: Prefect, tomorrow morning you

are meeting with the Compulsor to discuss the recent thefts of collected taxes by the desert dwelling zealots.

PILATE: Yes. Thank you.

SECRETARY SEPTIMUS: Of course. Good evening, Prefect.

The secretary moves to withdraw from the room.

PILATE: Septimus.

SECRETARY SEPTIMUS: Yes Prefect?

Pilate hesitates. He looks atypically unintentional and uncertain. Septimus has seen this look before.

SECRETARY SEPTIMUS: Zarah, sir?

Pilate seems relieved of some heavy burden just to hear the name.

PILATE: (*chuckling*) Am I that obvious?

SECRETARY SEPTIMUS: Not at all, sir.

PILATE: Yes. Have her come at once.

SECRETARY SEPTIMUS: As you wish, Prefect.

The secretary withdraws and Pilate remains seated deep in thought.

EXT. DARK COBBLESTONE STREET - EVENING

Zarah enters, sulking, from a darkened stage left and stops under a shaft of light. She speaks to the audience.

ZARAH: Men. All the world seems to be about them. My father, whose reputation I have sullied. The Scribes, and Elders of the Temple, who uphold the sacred laws that I am to serve under. And Pilate, who summons my body, but knows not my soul. Men. Will I ever discover who I am beyond what they expect and want me to be? I dream one day to find a home that is more than just the abode of familiar faces. More than an arranged collection of bitter tasting affections, where the softness in lips never quite arrives to the heart.

She slinks off into a darkened stage right.

INT. PREFECT PILATE'S PRAETORIUM OFFICE

Two roman legionnaires enter with Jesus of Nazareth in custody. The lead legionnaire presents Jesus to Pilate.

LEAD LEGIONNAIRE: Prefect, by order of arrest we have seized Jesus of Nazareth.

PILATE: *(to Jesus)* So, you are Jesus of Nazareth?

Jesus does not respond, and after a moment the legionnaire shoves him from behind.

LEAD LEGIONNAIRE: Answer the Prefect!

Jesus stumbles forward but does not respond. Pilate approaches Jesus, and looks closely in his eyes. Jesus stares ahead, eyes unfocused on anything.

PILATE: Is he deaf?

LEAD LEGIONNAIRE: No Prefect.

Pilate continues to examine his face.

PILATE: Has he spoken?

LEAD LEGIONNAIRE: He spoke at his arrest. One of his followers attacked a Centurion with a dagger.

PILATE: At his command?

LEAD LEGIONNAIRE: No Prefect. He in fact rebuked the zealot for attacking.

PILATE: Did he? What did he say to the assailant?

LEAD LEGIONNAIRE: He told him that if he chose to live by the sword he would die by it.

Pilate smiles and nods his head in affirmation.

PILATE: *(to Jesus)* No truer words were ever spoken, Nazarene.

Jesus looks up at Pilate and for the first time there is a connecting between the two men. Pilate recognizes the moment.

PILATE: Leave me with this man.

The Legionnaires nod and leave the room. Pilate walks over to a vessel of water.

PILATE: Can I offer you some water?

Jesus looks over at Pilate without expression.

PILATE: You look parched.

CHRIST: You recognize thirst, but mine is not for water.

PILATE: From silence to eloquence.

Pilate pours himself some water.

PILATE: The Sanhedrin seem to think you thirst for power. 'King of the Jews,' however...not too ambitious.

Jesus does not respond.

PILATE: Have you nothing to say about your accusers?

CHRIST: They speak for themselves.

PILATE: Yes, and they speak against you. But they are not here now. It is time for you to testify on your own behalf.

Jesus does not respond. Pilate puts the water chalice down and approaches Jesus.

PILATE: It is a serious enough matter these accusations. Understand I am not interested in condemning innocent men. I have the power to release you and end the matter.

CHRIST: Your authority is from Caesar.

PILATE: *(laughing)* Is it not sufficient?

Jesus looks directly at Pilate.

CHRIST: It is nothing to me.

PILATE: Ahhh. An honest Jew. That is refreshing. Fair

enough. I'd probably feel the same if our roles were reversed, though I don't think I would have the gall to speak as you do to a Roman Prefect.

There is a moment as Pilate attempts to stare down Jesus with this comment. Jesus engages his directness back and without fear. It becomes obvious to Pilate that there will be no intimidating this man.

PILATE: Caiaphas seems to think that you are planning some sort of overthrow of the Republic. Is that true?

CHRIST: The kingdoms of men will destroy themselves in due course without my assistance.

Pilate is taken aback by this response. He ponders the depth of the statement. He circles Christ.

PILATE: Rome as well? She too shall destroy herself?

Jesus looks directly at Pilate.

CHRIST: Ask your Caesar.

PILATE: *(cavalierly)* Tiberius will say Rome is sanctioned to rule the world. Hardly to wither and die.

CHRIST: And what say you Prefect?

Pilate steps away from Jesus and speaks to the air.

PILATE: *(more genuinely)* I say what I must, Nazarene.

CHRIST: Say what you must then unto the citizens of Caesar. I say what I must then unto the children of God.

PILATE: Hmmm. So you do speak on God's behalf as you are accused of.

Jesus does not respond.

PILATE: "I and God the Father are One." Did you say this?

CHRIST: Yes.

PILATE: This is the heresy and blasphemy accusation given to me by the Sanhedrin. "I and God are one." Ergo, you, Jesus of Nazareth, claim to be God.

CHRIST: It is a provocative logic. You may have it if it serves you.

PILATE: I'm just trying to understand.

CHRIST: So you say.

Pilate throws his arms up in the air.

PILATE: My mind is open, Nazarene.

Jesus stares straight ahead not looking at Pilate.

CHRIST: How open is a mind when it prefers its own thoughts?

PILATE: What is it with you? I have told you I am listening.

CHRIST: Are you with me, or against me?

PILATE: Why do you ask me this question, "Are you with me or against me"?

CHRIST: Is this not the question you mean to ask me on behalf of your Emperor?

Jesus looks directly at Pilate now for emphasis.

CHRIST: For though you may listen for an eternity, I have no answer to give you.

PILATE: I have a mind of my own outside of Caesar. I am talking to you now, not Tiberius.

CHRIST: You are a Roman first, are you not? Truly, of what need has Rome to listen to the thoughts of a Jewish carpenter from Galilee?

Pilate is appalled at this chastising.

PILATE: *(lowly, almost to himself)* No man speaks to me like this.

Christ looks down to the floor at his feet. Pilate "Hmmphs" to himself.

PILATE: You are bold, Nazarene. Perhaps a bit too bold.

Pilate pauses reflectively.

PILATE: But your assessment is fair, I am here to determine if you are any threat to Rome.

CHRIST: And what have you determined?

Pilate laughs genuinely at this comment. He shrugs his shoulders.

PILATE: That you embrace some sort of rebellious philosophy that appears to be of some concern to your accusers. That is all.

CHRIST: Is it mere philosophy to say that one man has as much access to the truth as any other man? Rebellious to claim that all people are worthy of dignity and respect, regardless of caste, creed or past transgressions?

Pilate frowns.

PILATE: Hmmm. You were actually somewhat interesting to me before this weary comment; bemoaning the rhetoric of the less privileged. If all were equal, then we wouldn't have an empire led by Roman office.

Pilate opens his arms in a gesture of solidarity.

PILATE: Let us not talk falsely; you seem intelligent. The Republic leads mostly because too many people follow.

CHRIST: To what scales have you access that lend the weight of divine favor toward a ruling Roman elite above all others?

PILATE: Scales? Is it not the law of nature? Look about you, man. The beasts of the world submit daily to the survival of the fittest, the strongest, the fiercest. My scales, and those of Rome, are drawn from the observation of nature itself.

CHRIST: Are we not as men gifted some greater perception

than the unmindful creatures of this world? Is our vision so base that we cannot see beyond the tooth and the claw? Roman Prefect, exalted among men, how curious that you elevate yourself no higher than by comparison with the primitive instincts that drive the beasts of this earth.

PILATE: Reason and logic drive my argument, Jew, hardly a bestial exposition.

CHRIST: And yet your gift of reason has no greater refinement of faculty than that of the baboon and the camel, spitting and screeching to achieve dominance over the pack.

PILATE: *(dismissively)* Most men are baboons. Is it not appropriate?

CHRIST: It certainly explains why you treat them that way.

PILATE: Is it my responsibility to elevate the ignorant of this world? It is enough that I must enforce order in Judea, so these tribal mongrels don't end up slaughtering each other day in and day out over a pinch of salt or a bucket of water.

CHRIST: And your form of violence is more noble then theirs?

Pilate laughs and shakes his head.

PILATE: *(exasperated)* I really should kill you for your audacity alone, you know that?

CHRIST: You murder on a whim, and call me audacious?

PILATE: *(fed up now)* Enough! Behold my restraint, Nazarene.

Pilate walks over to his desk trying to clear his head. He takes a deep breath to resume his composure.

PILATE: I am going to have you held. Mostly for your own protection. I do not trust Caiaphas and his Sanhedrin rabble. You understand?

Jesus does not respond.

Pilate shakes his head in frustration and approaches Jesus, looking at him intently.

PILATE: If I were not the sanctioned authority in this city he would already have you crucified with his own hands.

Pilate looks searchingly into Jesus' eyes.

PILATE: Where is your sense of fear, Nazarene? Every man should know a little fear when there is good reason.

CHRIST: Fear is as an estranged cousin to me. Though related through the flesh, we do not keep company.

Pilate frowns at this. He steps back and regards Jesus.

PILATE: Perhaps I should take heed of the council's concerns. A man without fear could build an empire as vast as Alexander.

CHRIST: Fear follows all worldly conquest, like the shadow of the emperor on parade.

Pilate turns away and speaks dramatically, as if to an audience before him.

PILATE: And now he suggests Alexander the Great suffered fear!

CHRIST: *(almost tauntingly)* No man can be called great who does not recognize that the only kingdom worth claiming is within.

Pilate chuckles at this.

PILATE: *(condescendingly)* Within? I mean no disrespect, but a man who is incapable of acquiring an estate in this world is hardly worth even recognizing.

CHRIST: Behold those who rise to conquer fear, Prefect, for they shall set the world free from every estate of tyranny.

Pilate is again taken aback, and he shakes his head.

PILATE: *(soberly)* Who are you?

CHRIST: Have not my accusers informed you?

PILATE: Your accusers are fools, useless temple rats, predictable as the tides. I know who they are.

He circles Jesus again then gets close to his face.

PILATE: But you...you make no sense to me. What are you after?

CHRIST: My heaven-sent inheritance has already been bestowed.

Pilate nods affirmatively.

PILATE: You dress pretty poorly for a man of such wealthy inheritance.

Jesus reaches out and in a bold act of extreme risk, touches the collar of Pilate's robe.

CHRIST: Luxurious clothing is often used to adorn the poor in spirit, is it not? Much in the same way that the ornate gold sarcophagi of the Pharaohs enshrine the dead rulers of Egypt.

Pilate is appalled that Jesus has touched his person. He grabs Jesus wrist and twists it into a painful submissive position. Jesus falls to his knees. Pilate holds the painful lock on Jesus' wrist, fuming as he glares down at him.

Jesus looks up at him, in pain, and breathing deeply but not showing anger or concern. There is a soft intensity in his eyes.

The two men stare at each other for several moments. Finally Pilate releases his hold.

PILATE: I am a Roman Prefect, Jew. Do not forget it.

Jesus rises. He is dignified as he looks at Pilate directly.

CHRIST: I have no worldly estate or title; the kind of man you do not even recognize. This, I shall not forget.

For the first time, Pilate begins to recognize that the type of man that is before him, he has no prior experience with.

PILATE: (calmly, almost respectfully) I have allowed for your words to cross certain boundaries with me, due to your obvious intellectual capacity; but you will keep your place in my presence.

CHRIST: (with authority) What is my place, Prefect?

Pilate finds no answer inside himself that feels true, and so he chooses to just end the conversation.

PILATE: We will discuss your circumstances tomorrow.

INT. PILATE'S BEDROOM CHAMBER - EVENING

Pilate sits on the edge of his large bed. Zarah is in a chair off to the side, awaiting her orders into the bed.

PILATE: Have you heard of this man they call Jesus of Nazareth?

ZARAH: I have.

PILATE: Has he a large following?

ZARAH: Many people like him.

PILATE: What say you?

ZARAH: I don't know him.

PILATE: What do the people you know say about him?

ZARAH: He preached with the Baptist. It is said he works miracles. Some believe he may be the Messiah.

PILATE: The Messiah? You Jews, and your precious Messiah. Has he rebels then among his following?

ZARAH: None I have heard of.

PILATE: What miracles do you refer to?

ZARAH: Healing the sick. Feeding multitudes where there was not food.

PILATE: Magic tricks.

ZARAH: It is said he has raised the dead.

PILATE: What?

ZARAH: A man who had died, Lazarus, it is said was commanded by Jesus to awaken, and they say that he did.

PILATE: From death? Do you believe it is so?

Zarah shrugs.

PILATE: Well, whatever it is they say he has done, the man seems to threaten no harm.

Zarah is not used to this verbal exchange. It is making her more nervous than the sickening routine she is at least used to. She wishes to get it over with.

ZARAH: Do you wish me to disrobe now?

Much to her shock, Pilate does not even respond to her. He now seems to be talking to himself about his moral dilemma.

PILATE: Why does the Sanhedrin desire to have this man crucified?

Pilate looks over at Zarah. She just shrugs.

Pilate shakes his head.

PILATE: Conspiracies seem to fester in this city among your people during Passover. My office will not play nursemaid to these intrigues.

INT. PREFECT PILATE'S PRAETORIUM OFFICE - DAY

Pilate looks up as the guard brings Jesus into the room. Pilate nods to the guard who turns and walks out, leaving Jesus and Pilate alone together.

PILATE: I am of a mind to release you. But I will ask you to leave Jerusalem at once, and not return.

Jesus does not respond.

PILATE: What say you?

CHRIST: Does the captor consult the captive?

Pilate sighs at this comment.

PILATE: Why make it hard for me to help you?

Jesus does not respond.

PILATE: You do know how painful crucifixion is, don't you?

CHRIST: There is pain everywhere in life, Prefect.

PILATE: Not like crucifixion. I have considered the proposition of putting to death a poor carpenter from Nazareth, and find I have no conviction for it.

Jesus smiles.

CHRIST: *(playfully)* The Prefect lacks conviction?

Pilate chuckles. Jesus' charm under these conditions is unique, and he appreciates it.

PILATE: Maybe I just don't want to kill you. Personally, I find your honesty, and intelligence, a bit refreshing.

Pilate walks over to the fountain and washes his hands symbolically.

PILATE: I deal with fools all day, and more fools in my dreams at night.

Pilate gazes out the window from the fountain.

PILATE: Everywhere fools.

Jesus looks over at Pilate. Pilate turns to face him.

PILATE: But not you. You are no fool, it's quite obvious. It also happens to be the reason why they want to kill you, Jesus of Nazareth. But I say, kill the sheep, not the sheepherder.

CHRIST: Does not the true shepherd die to save the flock?

PILATE: Perhaps, yet I will release you and you will return to Galilee. And I will wash my hands of this treason and blasphemy nonsense.

CHRIST: Some things must come to pass, Prefect.

Pilate flashes a look over to Jesus.

PILATE: Are you saying you won't leave Jerusalem?

Pilate walks up to Jesus. Jesus is not denying it.

PILATE: *(epiphany)* If I release you, you will continue to provoke Caiaphas and the temple priests. That is why you have come isn't it?

Jesus does not respond but we can feel his confirmation. Pilate moves to plan B.

PILATE: Fine. I will have you removed from the city - marched under guard back to Galilee.

CHRIST: I will only return to Jerusalem.

Pilate begins to cipher Jesus' intentions.

PILATE: You wish to be killed. Why?

He walks behind Jesus and leans forward near his ear.

PILATE: What is it you wish to die for? What is your cause Nazarene?

CHRIST: I live only for the Truth.

Pilate steps away from Jesus.

PILATE: Truth? This is a Roman virtue, Jew.

CHRIST: Ego Vox Veritatis.

PILATE: *(stunned)* More surprises...the carpenter is educated!

Pilate chuckles. Jesus does not respond. Pilate is intrigued. He is feeling a peer in his presence.

PILATE: This explains your scholarship; you studied abroad. Where? Persia? Babylon? Gaul? Mesopotamia? The Orient? Yes, you have that way about you.

Jesus does not reply.

PILATE: You are obviously no common Galilean. Are you even a Jew?

CHRIST: I live among the people of my heritage. Yet those who thirst for the Truth are my tribe, and wherever they are found, therein is my family.

Pilate nods. He begins to really recognize what is before him.

PILATE: Well, apparently you are no family to the priests. To them, I would wager, you are even more dangerous than a wilderness preacher like the Baptist.

CHRIST: They condemn what they don't understand. The practice is not uncommon among men.

Pilate turns away from Jesus and speaks to the air.

PILATE: Yet you are far more intelligent than the priests. You should be revered by them. But you are here instead, placed before me like a swine for slaughter. Fools hang these accusations around your neck. And fools insist I crucify you for them. But I will not kill such a man, and certainly not on a fool's request.

CHRIST: It is already written.

Pilate spins and faces Jesus.

PILATE: On this point you are mistaken my friend. I write the history in this jurisdiction.

Pilate summons two palace guards.

PILATE: *(to the guards)* Guards, put this man back in his cell.

PALACE GUARD 1: Yes, sir.

ACT II

INT. PILATE'S BEDROOM CHAMBER - NIGHT

Pilate prepares himself for bed when suddenly there is a commotion coming from the hallways outside.

Pilate looks over toward the doorway and in a moment his wife Claudia comes striding into the chamber, Septimus following.

PILATE: *(astonished)* Claudia! What are you doing here?

SECRETARY SEPTIMUS: Prefect, I am sorry. I had no notice of her arrival.

CLAUDIA: Is the Jewish girl here?

PILATE: What?

CLAUDIA: Don't lie to me. I don't care if she is, just get her out of the room now that I am here.

PILATE: No one is here but me, Claudia.

Claudia looks around suspiciously. She moves over to a seat and begins taking off her outer travelling garments.

Pilate waves off Septimus who is relieved to vacate.

CLAUDIA: Hmmph. Did you tire of her already? Word has it she is the fairest in all of Jerusalem. I too was a beautiful girl like her once, do you remember?

Pilate knows better than to say a word right now.

CLAUDIA: You should. You plucked me out of all the girls in Macedonia to be your perfect wife. Unfortunately for you, I aged.

PILATE: Claudia, what.....?

CLAUDIA: *(interrupting)* You men never learn, the beauty you are trying to capture all the time doesn't exist. It's only in your head. You're chasing shadows.

She looks over at him for emphasis.

CLAUDIA: That's all it is. Shadows that fade over time.

PILATE: Claudia, why have you come to Jerusalem? You should have stayed at home in Caesaria, I have told you that Passover is a dangerous time here.

CLAUDIA: How old is she? Seventeen, I hear. She probably likes having sex with you about as much as I do. Poor girl.

She scoops at the air in front of her nose.

CLAUDIA: I can smell her.

She walks over to Pilate at the edge of the bed.

CLAUDIA: I know what goes on.

She climbs past him onto the bed, and flops down and sighs, quite road-weary.

CLAUDIA: I hate this city. Of all the filthy, flea-infested, rat holes in the empire, you have to preside over Jerusalem. This city's only industry is piety. It produces nothing but a holy arrogance that reeks all the way to the Mediterranean. It's no wonder this blighted outpost is forever the bastard child of the empire.

PILATE: Well, my dear, why come all this way to subject yourself to the horrors of Jerusalem? Surely it was not to try and catch me in bed with...

CLAUDIA: (*interrupting*) Don't speak her name.

Pilate takes a deep breath.

PILATE: Claudia. Why have you come here?

She composes herself.

CLAUDIA: You have arrested a man. A Jew from Nazareth.

Pilate frowns

PILATE: Yes.

20

CLAUDIA: He is condemned to the cross?

PILATE: How do you know about this man?

CLAUDIA: He has come to me in my dreams, Pontius.

Pilate rolls his eyes. He has heard these paranormal ranting before from his wife.

PILATE: More dreams Claudia?

CLAUDIA: For weeks now he has appeared to me in my sleep. In the last dream he hung from the cross at your order, dying on Golgotha.

PILATE: Why would you dream this?

CLAUDIA: You must not kill this man Pontius.

PILATE: You came all the way from Caesaria to tell me that?

CLAUDIA: I had to know if he was real.

PILATE: Claudia, you have never met him. How do you know this man in your dreams is the same man I have arrested?

CLAUDIA: His name is Jesus is it not?

PILATE: And who told you this?

CLAUDIA: No one. That is the man's name in my dreams.

Pilate decides to indulge her.

PILATE: So what does Jesus say to you in your dreams? "Go to Jerusalem and tell your husband to let me go?" Honestly, that doesn't really even sound like him.

CLAUDIA: He said nothing of the sort, Pontius.

PILATE: Okay. What did he say?

Claudia looks a little self-conscious for the first time.

CLAUDIA: Nothing...actually.

PILATE: I'm sorry. Did you say, "nothing"?

Claudia glares at Pilate.

PILATE: He must have told you his name.

CLAUDIA: He says nothing. I just know that is his name.

PILATE: He says nothing, and yet you come all the way here on his behalf? Why?

Claudia sits up in the bed.

CLAUDIA: Because of the way I felt in my dream.

PILATE: What did you feel, Claudia?

A few moments pass as Claudia's whole countenance changes. Her face softens and her eyes open wider as light begins to move in them.

CLAUDIA: Peace. Pontius, I felt so much peace.

PILATE: Peace...?

CLAUDIA: I was no longer bothered with all the awful things in this world. Not even you and your mistresses burdened me. I was strangely content with everything, just as it was. As it is.

She looks over at Pilate.

CLAUDIA: I wish I hadn't woken up. I wish I were still asleep, with him, and full of that feeling.

Claudia's face darkens. She pauses before she speaks.

CLAUDIA: *(gravely)* Then came the dream of him on the cross, dying at your command.

Pilate is disturbed by this accurate premonition. He turns away from Claudia so as not to reveal his anxiety, and speaks to the air.

PILATE: Does he speak from the cross?

CLAUDIA: *(almost whispering)* I tell you, he doesn't speak to me with words.

Pilate listens intently.

PILATE: Was there no message he gave you to bring to me?

CLAUDIA: None.

Pilate sobers up, and turns to face Claudia.

PILATE: Claudia, these are political matters. Sometimes even I don't like what it is that I have to do. This Jesus of Nazareth...

CLAUDIA: *(interrupting)* I ask you as my husband. Do not kill Jesus of Nazareth. It is a bad omen, Pontius. I fear for your safety if you kill this man.

Pilate is stopped by her conviction and sincerity. He moves to reassure her, and himself.

PILATE: I am Caesar's Prefect. I am well protected.

CLAUDIA: I am not concerned about your safety from men.

PILATE: Of what dangers do you speak of?

Claudia begins an intimate appeal to her husband.

CLAUDIA: Hear me now, Pontius. This man Jesus, I felt only love from him, as you might feel from a mother or a dear father. He is no criminal. It is not right by nature to kill such a man, and I don't want his blood on the hands of my husband, or my family.

After a moment he nods his head.

PILATE: I hear what you have said, Claudia. If it helps you to know, my heart is as at least as heavy as yours in this matter.

Pilate speaks to the air.

PILATE: In the morning you will return to Caesarea under guard. Jerusalem will not rest easy in the coming days.

Pilate looks over at Claudia.

CLAUDIA: Pontius...

Pilate throws up a hand to interrupt her.

PILATE: *(interrupting)* Nothing further. Though I have failed as a husband on perhaps too many counts, I at least will not fail to keep my wife safe from the uncivilized barbarism of this city during Passover. That is all, Claudia.

INT. EMPTY STAGE - SPOTLIGHT ON ZARAH:

ZARAH: Pilate is more like me now, caught between two worlds he cannot reconcile. To see him struggle this way; to know that he too can feel confusion and uncertainty, makes me feel almost equal to him. But I am again uneasy, because with every hour, the Prefect is losing control of something inside himself, and there is no power at his disposal, nothing in all of Rome, that can soothe him, including me.

INT. PREFECT PILATE'S PRAETORIUM OFFICE - DAY

Pilate sits in his chair drinking, and though he is not "fall down drunk," the alcohol has loosened him up.

PILATE: I summoned you here to talk to you. I have a confession, Nazarene.

Pilate gestures at all the "Roman" environment around himself.

PILATE: I don't really believe... any of this. And yet, I have not the courage to say so publicly. You see, I am loathe to relinquish my lavish lifestyle.

Pilate takes a large drink form the wine challis.

PILATE: What say you?

CHRIST: You seek my judgment?

PILATE: This office is occupied by a man who is not in love with his own estate. I do not deserve this station. I know that you understand what I am saying.

CHRIST: Why not occupy your station in life Pilate? Whether you be a carpenter or a Prefect in the Roman Empire, it matters not.

PILATE: Because unlike you, my carpenter friend, I am a liar.

Pilate takes another swig of wine. Pilate begins to emotionally fold. He sinks down into his chair.

PILATE: I am unfit to serve Caesar. Maybe I should just join your followers.

CHRIST: Those that know only to follow, do so because they do not yet know themselves.

Pilate nods affirmingly. Suddenly a grave look comes over his face.

PILATE: What do you suppose will become of your followers when you are gone?

CHRIST: They must find the truth within themselves, no matter where I am.

Pilate points his finger at Jesus.

PILATE: But they won't will they? They will fall into despair without you. They will hang on everything you say while you are among them, but when you are gone, they will feel empty inside, and lose their way.

Pilate leans forward for emphasis.

PILATE: And I know this to be true. I think this is the actual reason I can't bring myself to condemn you.

Pilate looks away and shakes his head in shame.

PILATE: It isn't even your life I'm trying to save; I'm keeping you around to soothe my own wretched existence.

CHRIST: This honesty alone could be your salvation, Pilate. And it requires nothing from me.

Pilate looks over at Jesus while shaking his head.

PILATE: Honesty, I have tried. I have pled guilty to my weaknesses, disclosing to the heavens this darkness inside, confessing all before the ears of the divine.

Pilate's eyes well up with tears.

PILATE: But nothing comes back to me. The gods are silent.

CHRIST: Yet this is the beginning.

PILATE: The beginning of what? I have no idea where to begin anymore.

CHRIST: Nor did we as children, and yet we began.

PILATE: I am not a child anymore. I determine my fate as a man.

CHRIST: Your manly determinations will only encircle and squeeze the life out of you, Pilate. Make your choices as the children do, simply, and from the heart.

PILATE: Surely life is not to be lived as a child.

CHRIST: Consider what got lost in the process of becoming a man.

PILATE: Lost? What did I lose?

Jesus smiles and sits down.

CHRIST: There is the story of the boy whose favorite toy accidentally got lost, and ended up in the yard of the mean-spirited old man next door. There it sat, season after season, covered in dust, and stuck between the mean old man and his vicious dog. Too afraid to retrieve the special toy, the boy in time came to believe that he had outgrown it anyway. Many, many years later, the boy, now a man, came back to settle the estate of his parents and claim his portion of the inheritance from among his siblings. Looking over the wall to the neighbor's yard, he remembered the fear that once gripped him as a child, but the vicious dog and the mean old man had long since passed. Squinting at the untended yard, he noticed his magical toy, still half-buried in the ground. Tears came into his eyes and he quickly jumped over the wall and reclaimed his childhood treasure from the earth. He walked away in abiding joy, and never looking back, left the estate of his parents to his siblings to divide.

PILATE: I lost a child's toy?

CHRIST: You lost what it means to feel love, and the wonder of it.

PILATE: So love will make me a man?

CHRIST: Pilate, to truly love, is to die a man and wake up as God.

Pilate becomes very calm. The story is strange to his ear, but somehow soothing. He wants now to stop being caught in his own emotions and focus on Jesus.

PILATE: How can I help you, Jesus of Nazareth?

CHRIST: (*calmly*) Put me to death, Prefect.

Pilate slides back into anxiety.

PILATE: I cannot.

CHRIST: It will eventually come to pass.

PILATE: Then let your God come to my office and condemn you. Let him sentence you to death. I will have none of it.

Jesus stands up and approaches Pilate.

CHRIST: You may put me before my own people then, and let them judge me.

Pilate momentarily pieces together some sense of the power of his office.

PILATE: What? I am the ruler of law in this land, not a mob of Jews in the street.

CHRIST: Offer me in place of a Passover crucifixion. Is it not customary?

PILATE: On what Roman charge? I have only allegations of religious blasphemy levied against you by Jewish priests.

CHRIST: Prefect, you are a Roman officer, surely you

27

understand that in the world of men, formal indictments mean very little. It is the heat of emotion around the accusation that drives the nail into the wood, is it not?

Pilate knows this well. He nods cynically. He considers the request.

PILATE: You will submit to the judgment of your people?

CHRIST: Yes.

PILATE: Even if they release you?

CHRIST: Yes.

PILATE: You will be put before the general public to decide, not the priests.

CHRIST: Of course.

Pilate moves to clarify his position.

PILATE: I will tell them that I find no fault with you. I will not lie.

CHRIST: So be it.

Pilot nods.

PILATE: I will make the arrangements then. And if you are freed, you will leave Jerusalem and not return. I have your word?

CHRIST: You have my word. I will leave Jerusalem and not return if I am delivered from their judgment.

Pilate nods. He feels relieved from a terrible burden.

PILATE: Agreed.

INT. EMPTY STAGE - SPOTLIGHT ON ZARAH

ZARAH: Pilate has stopped taking my body when he summons me. He wants only my ears to listen to him now, and I know he wants my heart to care too, but I feel numb. I take no pleasure in his pain, I simply can't bring myself to take care of it. I suppose I should feel something for Pilate because he is finally being sincere. His change has made me curious about Jesus. I want to know what this man has done or said to Pilate to suddenly make him appear human.

INT. CHRIST'S PRISON CELL

Jesus sits quietly in his cell facing the wall. In a moment Zarah slinks over to the door and peers in. Jesus senses her there and speaks without looking over at her.

CHRIST: Hello, Zarah.

Zarah is surprised. She speaks in low tones so as not to be overheard

ZARAH: How do you know me?

CHRIST: (*looking at her*) Is it not common for one prisoner to recognize another?

ZARAH: I am not a prisoner like you...though I would gladly trade places with you.

Jesus does not respond.

ZARAH: I hate my life.

CHRIST: Why have you come to me?

ZARAH: I wanted to meet you before they...

Zarah realizes how insensitive her statement is, and chooses not to finish it. Jesus nods his head affirmatively knowing what she meant to say. Zarah redirects.

ZARAH: You changed Pilate.

CHRIST: Pilate changed himself, if he has changed at all.

ZARAH: He loves you. And Pilate loves no one but Pilate.

CHRIST: Not even you?

ZARAH: He uses me.

Jesus nods in understanding.

CHRIST: How has Pilate changed?

ZARAH: He stopped raping my body.

CHRIST: They may take our bodies. But they cannot possess who we are.

ZARAH: Pilate takes whatever he wants.

CHRIST: Is nothing beyond his reach?

ZARAH: Nothing. He is Caesar's Prefect.

CHRIST: Does he have your heart?

ZARAH: *(appalled)* He will never have my heart.

CHRIST: Verily. Some things even Caesar cannot own.

Christ looks toward the cell door.

CHRIST: When we know ourselves to be only those things which cannot be taken away by men, then we know more peace than suffering in this world.

ZARAH: *(disgusted)* Peace? Pilate has had his way with me since I was fourteen. This whole city murmurs daily about the disgrace I bring upon my family. I feel the judgment in their eyes burn into me wherever I walk. How many times I have been spit upon in contempt by women I cannot begin to even count. As for the men, I see the way they look at me, thinking I am a whore by choice. They would have me stoned if not for the fear of a brutal reprisal from Pilate. And when I am alone, I am left to my own sickening shame. I know no peace. I can't even imagine it anymore.

CHRIST: How long will you remain at this grave site mourning? Chained by choice to this headstone of guilt, feeling helpless and afraid?

ZARAH: *(cynically)* So this is what you do? Talk to people like you care.

Zarah grabs hold of the bars on the cell door and leans close.

ZARAH: You may fool Pilate, but you don't fool me. Without this locked door between us, you're an animal, just like the rest of them.

She shakes the cell door tauntingly.

ZARAH: The world would be better if all men were locked up in a cage like you.

Her hair falls over her face, and she stops to clear it away. Jesus looks over at the door.

Just then as both her hands are occupied clearing her hair away from her face, a clicking sound echoes into the cell, and the door UNLOCKS and cracks open on its own as she is standing in front of it.

A startled Zarah gasps and suppresses a scream while scrambling back against the wall in the hallway, breathing heavily.

Jesus quietly looks back down at the floor in front of his feet.

CHRIST: You are mistaken in your judgment of me daughter.

Zarah is scared but trying to take all of this in.

ZARAH: Did you do that?

Jesus does not respond. Zarah gathers herself. She sees that Jesus is making no attempt to get at her.

ZARAH: I have heard it said you have mystical powers.

She peels herself off the wall.

ZARAH: So it is true what they say about you.

Jesus looks over at Zarah.

CHRIST: No more true than what it is they say about you.

Zarah again approaches the cell door.

ZARAH: They say wicked things about me.

CHRIST: So then, they are mistaken on both counts.

Zarah feels emboldened, and she pushes open the door enough to slip inside the cell.

ZARAH: Are you here to deliver us from bondage?

CHRIST: Yes, but not as you imagine it.

Zarah looks at Jesus with curiosity.

ZARAH: Pilate is right, you are not like other men.

Zarah turns back around and looks at the cell door. She steps over and looks at the locking mechanism closely. Zarah opens the cell door wider. A look of crazed curiosity moves across her face. She looks over at Jesus.

ZARAH: Why do you not flee? Go, now. Or they will kill you!

Jesus stands up and walks over toward the front of the cell but does not leave. He stops in front of Zarah and looks at her compassionately. Zarah's teenaged emotions are running wild and all over the place.

ZARAH: You could do anything! You have powers. Why do you let them treat you this way?

A dark look of rage moves across her face now.

ZARAH: Does your magic have limits? You could turn Pilate's mind against him.

CHRIST: Pilate's mind has set a curse upon itself. He needs light, not more darkness.

Her eyes begin to well up with tears.

ZARAH: I hate him. I hate him.

CHRIST: You hate what has happened to you.

Zarah begins to weep.

ZARAH: I am ruined. Pilate has seen to that.

CHRIST: Those who know you may think otherwise.

Zarah drops her head down and her hair slides over her face.

ZARAH: No one really knows me.

Jesus pauses a moment and then reaches down and gently grabs her hand in his.

CHRIST: Those around you may fail to see who you truly are, but you have known since you were a child. Have you not?

She lifts her head and looks up at him.

ZARAH: I don't talk about such things.

CHRIST: Zarah, you are a daughter of God, and you have been gifted to know the deepest understandings.

Suddenly Zarah laughs as if possessed - this last piece is too much. She pulls her hand away from his and emotionally lashes out.

ZARAH: You are mad! I am a whore, deflowered by the Prefect himself. Your God makes poor choices.

Jesus does not respond. Zarah is trembling, tears streaming down her cheeks. She buries her face in her hands.

ZARAH: What does God want from me?

CHRIST: Just to listen.

ZARAH: Listen to what?

CHRIST: Something deeper than your anger.

She pulls her hands away and looks at him directly.

ZARAH: Anger is all I know.

CHRIST: Then know nothing for a while.

ZARAH: You say I am a daughter of God. My actual father is ashamed; cannot bear to even look at me. The truth is, that ugliness feels more real to me right now than your holy words.

Jesus smiles, and walks over to the cell door and inspects the lock mechanism for a few moments. Zarah looks at him questioningly. After a moment he looks back at her.

CHRIST: (*playfully*) I always say, "It's a good time to quit talking when they start calling you holy."

Zarah smiles and chuckles through her tears.

ZARAH: I'm sorry, I just kind of hate everything right now.

CHRIST: The mind cannot long hate what the heart makes clear. It will pass.

She walks over to the cell door where Jesus is and looks around nervously.

ZARAH: Pilate will punish me severely if he finds I am here with you.

CHRIST: And yet you came anyway.

ZARAH: I guess I did.

Zarah walks back over to the cell bench and sits down.

ZARAH: So, are you sent from God to be a great king as some people say?

Jesus walks over and sits down on the bench next to her.

CHRIST: Sister, I have no interest in the kingdoms of this world.

ZARAH: Will you destroy Rome's legions as the oral traditions foretell?

CHRIST: I am not anyone that has been prophesied about.

ZARAH: Yet it is written that one day the Messiah will come and deliver us.

CHRIST: Zarah, all scripture is as dead as the bones of my forefathers.

Zarah nods. She looks back over to the door and inquires more calmly now.

ZARAH: Why do you not escape given the chance?

Jesus looks over at the door and then back at Zarah.

CHRIST: There is only one prison we need escape from in this life, and it is of our own making.

Zarah gets up and walks across the cell to the open cell door.

ZARAH: The prophets say freedom from bondage will come through war, led by the Messiah.

CHRIST: In the ages of ignorance the violence will continue, but it will never lead to true freedom.

ZARAH: Will God not deliver us?

CHRIST: When men finally look to God, there will be salvation. But in these times, men cast their gaze only downward beneath the great tree of life. Under that sacred canopy, they behold the myriad shafts of broken light, everywhere in parts and mixed with shadows, dappled upon the ground. Never looking up to the heavens, men imagine the sun above, the one source of all light, to be in pieces as well. This is the fall of man, whom though born from whole light, have by innocent error become transfixed by the shadow play of creation, fearfully obsessing over the dramatic displays of dark and light. Mankind will continue to wage war, until they recognize that prior to all shadows, there is only one Light.

ZARAH: There is heaven, and there is earth. It is taught that the two do not mix.

CHRIST: And yet in me there is no such division. I and the Creator of the cosmos are realized as One.

ZARAH: I have never heard anyone talk like you do.

CHRIST: One day, others will say the same about you.

ZARAH: Who would ever listen to what I have to say?

CHRIST: More even than have listened to me, sister. Many will love you; but some will revile you, and condemn you twofold: First, because you bear witness to the truth, and second because you are a woman.

ACT III

EXT. PILATE'S PRAETORIUM BALCONY - DAY

Pilate stands and addresses the crowd in the praetorium courtyard below.

PILATE: Citizens of Rome, you have been summoned to decide the case of Jesus of Nazareth. He is accused by the Sanhedrin Council of inciting rebellion as a self-proclaimed king of the Jewish people. The Roman State has no evidence against him save the accusations of the temple priests, and the accused himself makes no such claims to me. As is customary at Passover, however, he may be crucified, at your judgment, in place of the justly convicted criminal Barrabas. How say you, the people?

Pilate summons his Captain to bring forward Jesus to the balcony edge.

As the Captain brings Jesus forward to the edge, almost immediately the crowd begins to YELL out.

CROWD: (O.S.) Death to Jesus! Crucify Him!

Pilate is stunned by the crowd's illogical cruelty. He turns to his guard Captain sensing something a foul.

PILATE: I told them I find no fault in this man. How is it they condemn him to the cross?

The Captain offers no explanation.

CROWD: (O.S.) Death to Jesus! Free Barrabas! Death to Jesus, Free Barrabas!

Pilate looks down again at the crowd in astonishment, but suddenly something catches his eye. Pilate notices Sanhedrin Pharisees in the shadows goading on the crowd to condemn Jesus. Pilate explodes with rage.

PILATE: Priests!

Pilate points to the culprits in the crowd.

PILATE: *(to the Captain)* The priests poison the crowd!
   Captain, have your men arrest them. Bring them to me now.

The Captain moves across the veranda to give the order to the two posted GUARDS under his command. The Guards move off to arrest the priests.

Pilate is fuming, and he looks over at Jesus. Jesus speaks to him calmly.

CHRIST: It is decided.

Ignoring Jesus' words, Pilate yells to the Captain, directing him to take Jesus away.

PILATE: Captain! Get him out of here.

The Captain takes Jesus away.

Pilate leans back over the balcony, waiting to observe the guards seize the Pharisees.

PILATE: *(to the crowd assembled)* By order of the Prefect, disband this gathering of fraud!

INT. EMPTY STAGE - SPOTLIGHT ON ZARAH

ZARAH: I had seen the desperation in Pilates eyes on so many nights, and I know now what it was that drove him to the dark deed. It seems like it is only a matter of time before lost men like him become takers in this life. Jesus didn't take things. He was full with something that sustained him from somewhere else, and so he gave instead. That is what set him apart, made him free and alive in a way that I wanted to be. Jesus, in a prison cell. Pilate, the emperor's right hand. Who was the real prisoner? Who had the true authority?

INT. PREFECT PILATE'S PRAETORIUM OFFICE

There is a commotion as the captain brings in the four seized Pharisee priests. Pilate is fuming and he launches into them.

PILATE: Manipulators! You dare mock my office?

VOCAL PRIEST: Prefect, we sought only to levy our opinion on the matter.

Pilate pounces on the vocal priest and seizes him by the throat. The other priests all GASP.
Pilate zeroes in on the offending priest he has by the throat. His eyes seem murderous.

PILATE: (through his teeth) Do you think I am a fool?

Pilate's powerful forearms feed the fury of his choke-hold. The Priest is nearly passed out when Pilate releases his hold, letting air finally return to the priest's lungs. The Priest GAGS and COUGHS, trying to recover.
Pilate scans the room now for his true target.

PILATE: I see the lead jackal is not among you.

Pilate walks over to the door and glances back at the Pharisee priests with contempt.
Pilate speaks eerily low and deliberate to the lead guard.

PILATE: Get me Caiaphas.

Pilate leaves the room and as he walks out he murmurs to himself.

PILATE: That spineless puppet priest will answer to me.

INT. CHRIST'S PRISON CELL - DAY

Jesus sits inside his cell in meditative repose. Pilate arrives outside the cell and motions for the prison Guard to open the door. The prison Guard complies and Pilate enters the cell with Jesus.

PILATE: I had Caiaphas arrested.

CHRIST: Pilate, why do you pursue this matter?

PILATE: They condemned you falsely. The crowd that assembled to decide your fate was being puppeted by Sanhedrin henchmen in the crowd, priests inciting them to chant, "Death to Jesus." I heard it with my own ears, I saw it with my own eyes.

CHRIST: Even so, you agreed to fulfill their verdict.

PILATE: It was a conspiracy! The people were coerced by the priests.

CHRIST: What does it matter?

PILATE: I will not be manipulated by Jews.

CHRIST: This isn't about you.

Pilate throws his hands up in the air.

PILATE: What do you want from me?

CHRIST: I want you to keep your word.

PILATE: It was a mockery! And I protected you from it.

CHRIST: The storm is mine. I do not require your shelter from it.

Pilate sighs. He is exasperated. He squints at Jesus.

PILATE: Your private storm seems to be raining on all of us, Jesus of Nazareth.

Just then a commotion is heard down the corridor outside the cell, and Pilate glances back outside the cell. The Captain appears with a struggling Caiaphas in tow.

CAPTAIN: Prefect, we deliver Caiaphas to you as ordered.

The distraction is welcome to Pilate's frustration. He glances back at Jesus.

PILATE: This is between Caiaphas and me now.

Pilate turns away from Jesus and glares through the bars at Caiaphas in the corridor for several moments without speaking. For a moment there is only the intense stare down of Pilate directed at Caiaphas. Finally he addresses the Captain.

PILATE: *(evenly)* Lock him up. I am coming.

The Captain shoves Caiaphas on down the corridor. Pilate looks back at Jesus.

CHRIST: You understand you are serving no one but yourself right now.

PILATE: *(gravely)* It must be nice for you to have a God to serve. Most of us are just stuck with ourselves.

Pilate leaves the cell to follow the Captain who is locking up Caiaphas.

INT. CAIAPHAS' PRISON CELL - EVENING

Caiaphas is shoved in the cell and Pilate enters behind him. The Captain waits outside.

Pilate paces the cell slowly like a lion circling its meal.

PILATE: Is it not against your religion to gamble, Priest?

Caiaphas does not respond. He knows this meeting is not about conversation.

PILATE: And yet, you gamble with me.

Pilate leans into Caiaphas and whispers for affect.

PILATE: I know what you're thinking. You wager that Caesar will not approve of the unauthorized killing of a high priest by some hot-headed Prefect.

Pilate steps back, and opens his arms.

PILATE: Well...place your bet here, in Judea, under my jurisdiction, Priest. And I will tell you that in spite of all the law and order I maintain, accidents happen. Tragic things. Things that you don't have to explain to anybody.

Pilate moves into the face of Caiaphas until they are nose to nose.

PILATE: *(slowly for emphasis)* Never gamble with me again, Priest. You will lose that bet. And you will lose even more than you have to wager. You have my word on that.

Pilate reaches up and grabs hold of the priest's tunic and dislodges it slightly from its traditional seating upon the head, just to humiliate him further.

Pilate steps away and looks at the tunic now sitting askew on Caiaphas' head.

PILATE: Accidents can happen.

Pilate walks over toward the door and orders the Captain.

PILATE: *(to the Captain)* Move him into the cell with Jesus.

INT. CHRIST'S PRISON CELL - EVENING

The Captain grabs Caiaphas and thrusts him into the cell with Jesus and shuts the door. Pilate speaks from outside.

PILATE: Joseph Caiaphas, chief priest of the Sanhedrin, I trust you recognize Jesus of Nazareth. The man whom you are trying so hard to have my office murder on your behalf. I will have you know that there is no case against the man under Roman law for execution, which leaves one empty cross on Golgotha tomorrow morning.

Pilate steps up close to the cell, half smiling now.

PILATE: Yet there is perhaps a new candidate. Enjoy your good company Priest. It may be your last.

Pilate leaves, laughing to himself.

INT. CHRIST'S PRISON CELL - NIGHT

Jesus smiles.

CHRIST: Hello, Joseph.

Caiaphas shakes his head in disgust. He looks out the cell door to ensure Pilate is out of earshot.

CAIAPHAS: He is gone mad.

Caiaphas looks over at Jesus.

CAIAPHAS: A Roman prefect wouldn't dare kill the high priest of Judea without direct order from Caesar. There would be unending rioting in the streets. Pilate will come to his senses and release me from this stinking cell.

CHRIST: You are a prisoner of your own robes, Caiaphas, inside or outside of this...

Jesus sniffs at the air playfully.

CHRIST: ...Fragrant cell.

Caiaphas walks into the cell and sits across from Jesus with a look of contempt on his face. Caiaphas now transforms his fear into a disgust, directed at Jesus.

CAIAPHAS: And you. Why have you come among us? Do you think your message of heaven on earth suits these times? Tell me, does it look like heaven to you out there in the streets, Rabbi?

CHRIST: Your eyes are enslaved, Joseph. To you the streets appear wicked because the mind that regards them is thus.

CAIAPHAS: Of course, you have the vision of God, Emmanuel. Compared to you, I am just a blind man, groping at symbols.

Caiaphas laughs cynically. He begins pacing around the cell dramatically.

CAIAPHAS: I have but one question for you, oh great sage. Of what use are you to the people? Do you think your doctrine of direct experience of God will ever take hold with the ignorant you preach to?

CHRIST: Joseph, for whom do you put on this exhibition? It is just you and I in this cell.

CAIAPHAS: Mikra doctrine is no exhibition.

CHRIST: The old laws, like your Sanhedrin robes, are spectacle. Where is the life in them?

CAIAPHAS: You blaspheme our sacred religion. There is no end to your heresy!

CHRIST: We both know that my testimony is not about your religion.

CAIAPHAS: (mockingly) And yet you come to the Temple at Passover with your message of mystical salvation.

CHRIST: What better place than a prison to preach freedom, Joseph?

CAIAPHAS: Freedom. Listen to you. Where is your ministry of liberation after you are gone, Jesus of Nazareth? Among your ragtag group of weak-willed followers? You are just a passing intrigue, a novelty. We are the religion of the one true God, whose doctrine has been held sacred for 2000 years since Abraham. Who do you think you are to usurp our traditions?

Jesus smiles genuinely.

CHRIST: Does Yahweh share your contempt of me, Caiaphas?

Caiaphas walks over to the cell door and peers out.

CAIAPHAS: Just like the Baptist you are, insolent to the end.

Caiaphas looks back over at Jesus again directly.

CAIAPHAS: Your zealot ministry will soon be buried with your body, and forgotten. Mark my words, Rabbi.

INT. PREFECT PILATE 'S PRAETORIUM OFFICE - EVENING

Pilate sits quietly in thought when suddenly there is a commotion in the halls leading up to his office.

A single Centurion enters with a man in his custody. The two men enter Pilate's chamber.

SINGLE CENTURION: Prefect, as you requested, Judas Iscariot.

Pilate nods.

PILATE: Come in, Judas. Have a seat.

Pilate looks over to the single Centurion.

PILATE: *(to the Centurion)* You may leave us now.

Judas sits down nervously. The Centurion leaves.

PILATE: Rough night for the loyal followers of Jesus?

Judas nods apprehensively.

PILATE: It won't get any better tomorrow.

JUDAS: Have I been arrested?

PILATE: I am told that you met with the temple priests before leading my legionnaires to Jesus. I want to ask you some questions.

Judas says nothing, not knowing what to expect.

PILATE: Did they pay you to betray Jesus to the legionnaires?

JUDAS: No. I mean I was offered silver, yes, but I didn't take it.

PILATE: Was it specifically Caiaphas who bribed you with the silver?

JUDAS: Yes sir, 30 pieces. But like I said, I didn't want it.

Pilate nods, pleased at garnering some criminal testimony against Caiaphas.

PILATE: And so what are your reasons for betraying your beloved Jesus?

Judas looks away trying not to show the emotion he obviously feels inside.

Pilate stops and considers his assumption. He leans back in his chair.

PILATE: I'm sorry, maybe you have no such affection for the man.

JUDAS: I do care for him. It's just that I care also for the cause that many of us hold sacred.

PILATE: What cause is that?

JUDAS: Exposing the corruption in the House of Herod, and that of the Sanhedrin.

PILATE: So why assist Priests in the arrest of Jesus?

JUDAS: He does not represent the cause that John the Baptist began with our people.

PILATE: Was Jesus not a friend of the Baptist?

JUDAS: They were cousins. He loved John. But John was different than Jesus. John understood and hated the corruption among our people. He spoke out against the temple priest hypocrites, and exposed Herod Antipas for the tyrant that he is.

PILATE: Is the message not the same between the cousins?

JUDAS: The Baptist preached against the corruption amongst our people, and taught us that we should go out and change it. Jesus teaches us to take responsibility for the error of our own ways, and that we should just change ourselves.

PILATE: And for this he should be condemned?

JUDAS: I thought maybe he might be jailed or detained for some period, that's all.

PILATE: Can his philosophy not coexist with your movement?

JUDAS: Many that once followed John now follow Jesus. But Jesus dilutes the movement.

PILATE: Does he?

JUDAS: Jesus says his kingdom is not of this world. I say that his heavenly kingdom does not deal with Herod or Caiaphas.

PILATE: Indeed.

Judas sighs deeply.

PILATE: Why not tell him how you feel?

JUDAS: He knows. It is no secret between us.

Pilate nods.

PILATE: You understand he will be crucified in the morning?

Judas is genuinely stunned to hear this.

JUDAS: But he has committed no Roman crime.

PILATE: Did you not know this might come to pass when you revealed him to the legionnaires?

Judas shakes his head.

JUDAS: Jesus knew it more than any of us; that he would be condemned to death. He told us as much at our last supper together.

PILATE: (*almost to himself*) And so he tells me now.

JUDAS: What?

PILATE: Nothing.

Pilate takes a deep breath.

PILATE: Do you regret what you have done, Judas?

Judas drops his head in shame.

JUDAS: Yes.

He looks up at Pilate, almost appealing to him.

JUDAS: But this was going to happen to Jesus no matter what. I know it was wrong what I did, but....

Judas seems to get disoriented in his thinking, and he can't seem to put the words together.

PILATE: What?

JUDAS: *(struggling)* I know it sounds strange, but I almost feel like he was counting on me to do it somehow; depending on me to betray him to the authorities. Like it was all just part of some pre-ordained plan.

Judas drops his head again.

JUDAS: I can't explain it.

Pilate nods his head affirmingly.

PILATE: You don't need to. Not to me.

INT. EMPTY STAGE - SPOTLIGHT ON ZARAH:

ZARAH: To be near Jesus was to be tossed around at sea by the powerful storm that was his ministry. Without ever asking directly, Jesus had somehow invited us to surrender everything in this life, like he himself had, to the God that made us all. I wondered, who among us was really ready for that? Who was prepared to be that free?

INT. PRISON CORRIDOR - EVENING

A Roman guard moves down the corridor that fronts Christ's prison cell on his way to release Caiaphas. The Roman guard opens the door to Jesus' cell and addresses Caiaphas.

ROMAN GUARD: Caiaphas, you are free to go.

The Roman guard leans over toward a cell a couple doors down with Barrabas in it.

ROMAN GUARD: Barrabas, you're next, be ready. Pilate has said two criminals go free this evening.

Caiaphas smiles. He gets up and looks over at Jesus with a satisfied contempt.

He walks out the prison cell door. The Roman guard grabs Caiaphas and shuts the door. He leads Caiaphas away.

In a moment there is a voice from outside of Jesus' cell.

BARRABAS: (V.O. *from the corridor*) So it is you who is to take my place on the cross tomorrow.

INT. JESUS' PRISON CELL - EVENING

Jesus walks over to the cell door.

CHRIST: Hello Barrabas.

INT. BARRABAS PRISON CELL - EVENING

Barrabas has his face pressed up to the bars of his cell.

BARRABAS: Unfortunate turn of events for you, brother.

INT. JESUS' PRISON CELL - EVENING

CHRIST: Fortune and misfortune are consummate lovers. There is not much use in separating them.

INT. BARRABAS: PRISON CELL - EVENING

BARRABAS: Jesus of Nazareth. I heard you preaching with John in Galilee. I liked the Baptist, he spoke his mind. But these are dangerous times to be free in thought, brother. Calling out Herod proved fatal for him. And now I see Caiaphas condemns you.

INT. JESUS' PRISON CELL - EVENING

Jesus likes Barrabas' sincerity and candor.

CHRIST: (*injecting levity*) I thought we had a nice visit, Joseph and I.

Barrabas laughs heartily.

BARRABAS: Ha! You wouldn't know it by the look on his face when he left!

INT. JESUS' PRISON CELL - EVENING

Jesus smiles.

CHRIST: He doesn't appreciate Pilate's accommodations as much as I do.

They both laugh.

INT. BARRABAS: PRISON CELL - EVENING

BARRABAS: Have you spoken out against the corruption within the Sanhedrin?

CHRIST: That corruption speaks loudly enough for itself. I find no need to echo the obvious.

BARRABAS: Well, you must have done something to offend Caiaphas.

CHRIST: Indeed. I spoke about God.

Barrabas laughs.

BARRABAS: Oh well, death to you! Yes, that would do it. Caiaphas is certain he owns that topic.

INT. JESUS' PRISON CELL - EVENING

Jesus chuckles. He is enjoying Barrabas.

INT. BARRABAS: PRISON CELL - EVENING

Barrabas shakes his head.

BARRABAS: Fools, Romans and Jews, are running all of Judea. The whole lot of them need to be overthrown! If I could do it myself I would.

INT. JESUS' PRISON CELL - EVENING

CHRIST: *(smiling)* Well, you certainly have the spirit for the undertaking, my friend.

BARRABAS: *(sighs)* Spirit? I fear I am just a vexation that gets louder with wine.

CHRIST: If this wine increases the volume of the just in heart, then let us all drink from your cup Barrabas.

INT. PRISON CORRIDOR

Just then the Roman Guard emerges in the hallway.

ROMAN GUARD: Let's go, Barrabas.

BARRABAS: *(to the guard)* Alright.

The Roman Guard reaches Barrabas' cell and opens the door. The two men walk down the corridor and when they reach Jesus' cell, Barrabas stops at Jesus' door.

BARRABAS: Brother, I am saddened that they will take your life tomorrow.

The Roman Guard pushes Barrabas onward but he grasps at the bars on Jesus' cell.

Barrabas turns toward the Roman Guard.

BARRABAS: *(to the Roman Guard)* Regard this man. How he fears not on the eve of his death. How he extends love to others in the very hour when all that is dear will be cruelly taken from him. He is neither bitter nor is he spiteful. Truly he is a better man than either of us.

The Roman Guard looks at Jesus, and Jesus at the Roman Guard. There is a moment of genuine mutual respect between the men before the Roman Guard collars Barrabas and forces him on down the corridor.

ACT IV

INT. PILATE'S BEDROOM CHAMBER - NIGHT

Pilate lies in bed, eyes wide open, unable to sleep. He rolls over and closes his eyes in one last attempt to fall asleep.

Moments later his eyes open. He sighs. There will be no sleep for him tonight.

He rolls out to the edge of the bed where Zarah lies sleeping, and whispers to her.

PILATE: Zarah.

Zarah awakens. She is on her side facing away from him.

ZARAH: What?

PILATE: I cannot sleep. The guilt is tormenting me.

She continues to speak with her back to him.

ZARAH: Why condemn him if you don't want to?

PILATE: I have to.

ZARAH: You are the Prefect of Judea. You have authority.

Pilate does not respond. After a few moments Zarah redirects the question with emphasis.

ZARAH: Why do you not release him?

Again there is no response. The tension is building. Zarah knows she has the matter by the throat, and she rolls over now to look at Pilate for emphasis.

ZARAH: You condemn a man you know to be innocent. It makes no sense.

Pilate looks at her, then drops his head onto the pillow, eyes fixed on the ceiling.

PILATE: No man I have come across, Jew or Roman, knows and accepts his destiny as this man does. Do you not understand? I respect him, Zarah. Even envy him in the strangest way. To be so near to his Maker. So close to his Creator as to have that God whisper intimately in his ear, "Die for me...die for me, Jesus." He wishes only to obey his God, and I must honor it.

ZARAH: But it is the Pharisees who condemn him.

PILATE: This is not about the Priests. It is not about Rome. It is about this man and the God that created him. Can no one see this but me?

Zarah knows Pilate is right, but she, too, is struggling with Jesus' death.

ZARAH: *(distantly)* Maybe he is mad. What kind of God asks you to die for him?

PILATE: The very same one that gave him life, it appears.

Zarah does not respond for a moment but then considers a new manipulative tact, and enters it halfheartedly.

ZARAH: Why would you respect a man who uses your office?

Pilate rolls over to face her.

PILATE: What are you talking about?

ZARAH: He wishes to martyr himself. To gain acclaim. It is so obvious. He could just as easily jump off the sheer side of Mount Gilboa and not include you in his death wish. He seeks fame by using the spectacle of the crucifixion through your office, can't you see that?

Pilate considers the accusation as he rolls over again onto his back and stares at the ceiling again.

PILATE: Caesar exploits this office everyday for the whims of his empire. If Jesus is also using my office then I suppose I am reconciled to being of service to those greater than I.

Zarah gives up trying to persuade him, she rolls away from him

*and puts her head down again on the pillow and closes her eyes.
After a few moments Pilate speaks to her.*

PILATE: I should not have summoned you here tonight. Go
home.

*Zarah's eyes open. She stares straight ahead. She cannot believe
she is hearing these words. For a moment she does not move. Then
slowly she rolls over and looks at him.*

ZARAH: What did you say?

Pilate looks at her directly.

PILATE: I said go home, Zarah.

*Zarah gets out of bed mechanically and quietly begins to put on
her clothes. There is silence in the room as she does.*

Pilate moves to the edge of the bed and sits upright on it.

When she finishes dressing she looks over at Pilate.

PILATE: *(assuring her)* It's late. I can arrange for a centurion to
escort you back to your family.

*The two look at each other without expression for several
moments.*

ZARAH: I have no family anymore, Prefect.

*Zarah walks out of the room to go home and Pilate tracks her with
his eyes as she leaves.*

INT. PRISON CORRIDOR

*The Night Guard stationed in the corridor just down from Jesus' cell
is picking something off of his helmet when suddenly there is the
SOUND of humming and chanting coming from one of the cells.*

*The Night Guard moves down the corridor to inspect the scene. He
stops in front of Jesus' prison cell where the sound is coming from.*

INT. CHRIST'S PRISON CELL

Jesus is sitting cross-legged on the floor. His upper torso is moving in rhythmic gyrations generating a circular pattern by using the base of his spine seated on the floor as a fulcrum for the movement.

His eyes are closed and his hair has fallen down forward from the concentric gyrations and it is obscuring most of his face.

He has an almost eerie smile as he HUMS and CHANTS intermittently.

Jesus is in fact in an ecstatic state, running energy up and down his spine utilizing a form of Kriya yoga practice.

The NIGHT GUARD is at the cell door peering inside at Jesus. He watches, curious about what he is seeing.

After several moments the night Guard moves to get his attention.

NIGHT GUARD: (whispering) Jew.

Jesus stops immediately. He slowly opens his eyes. Under the disheveled hair lying across his face we can see the wild eyes of a man on fire. This is a Jesus we have not seen before.

He stares intently at the night guard, and though he looks like a wild animal, he is extremely calm and present.

The night guard looks up and down the corridor for any other people.

NIGHT GUARD: (still whispering) They say you can heal the sick. Is it true?

Jesus continues to keep his eyes fixed on the Night Guard, but does not respond.

NIGHT GUARD: My son, he is very ill. They say he does not have long to live.

Again, Jesus does not respond.

NIGHT GUARD: I was wondering if you could...

Again the night guard looks for any other people around.

NIGHT GUARD: Heal him. He is very sick.

Jesus does not respond or move. The night guard is becoming increasingly anxious and desperate.

NIGHT GUARD: Did you not hear me? Why do you just sit there?

Jesus remains still, steely-eyed on the prison guard.

NIGHT GUARD: Damn you! Cure my son! You raise the dead, I know you can do it. Why don't you help?

Jesus remains still. The night guard starts to completely lose his composure. He grasps the cell door bars and presses his face into them.

NIGHT GUARD: Do something! Do you hear me, he is sick!

Jesus moves quickly from where he is seated and like a cat, in a moment is at the door inches from the face of the night guard. His wild eyes are even more intense now.

CHRIST: *(slowly for emphasis)* Your child is not sick. He was born *into* a sickness.

The night guard is somewhat taken at Jesus' directness.

NIGHT GUARD: What? What is this you say?

Jesus pulls himself closer to the bars and puts his hand slowly onto the forehead of the night guard.

CHRIST: The seed is indeed whole, yet the fruit that bears it has become spoiled.

Jesus pulls his hand off of the night guard's forehead as if he is extracting a wet wash cloth from a bucket.

CHRIST: If the child is to live, the father must be born again.

The night guard's previous rage instantly transforms into a deep grief and he begins to spontaneously WEEP.

Jesus steps back and points at the weeping night guard.

CHRIST: Seek ye no more the path of error.

The night guard falls to his knees sobbing inconsolably at the cell door.
Jesus turns away and settles back down into his previous meditative

repose, and closes his eyes.

The night guard's MOANING begins to create a commotion that attracts a second guard who comes running and arrives at the cell.

GUARD 2: What is going on here?

The night guard continues to sob on his knees. The second guard checks the cell door to make sure it is locked.

GUARD 2: *(to Jesus)* What have you done to him?

The second guard reaches down to the weeping night guard.

GUARD 2: What's happened? Are you hurt?

The night guard cannot stop sobbing. After checking the night guard for wounds the second guard is perplexed and confused at finding none. He leaves to report the incident.

Jesus begins to resume the cyclic movements as the night guard outside continues to sob.

After a moment Pilate comes down to the cell with the second guard. They arrive at the cell and Pilate assesses the situation.

PILATE: *(to the night guard)* What is it, man? Get up now!

The still sobbing night guard remains on the floor weeping inconsolably.

PILATE: *(to the second guard)* He is unhurt?

GUARD 2: He is not wounded anywhere.

PILATE: Get him out of here.

The second guard picks up the sobbing night guard and helps him walk off down the corridor. After they have departed Pilate looks into the cell.

PILATE: Jesus.

Jesus opens his eyes.

CHRIST: Pilate.

Pilate looks at Jesus questioningly, but then decides to just let the incident go. He would rather talk to Jesus personally.

PILATE: I cannot sleep.

Jesus nods.

PILATE: I was thinking to have some wine. Maybe that would help. Join me?

Jesus smiles and gets up. He approaches the door.

CHRIST: Caiaphas was right about one thing. This cell does stink a bit.

Pilate hesitates before opening the door.

PILATE: So I shouldn't ask what that was about?

Jesus smiles.

CHRIST: I wouldn't.

Pilot nods his head and smiles as he opens the door. Jesus steps out and Pilate puts his hand on Jesus' shoulder.

PILATE: It's good to know I'm not the only one you drive to tears.

Jesus smiles and the two walk off together.

INT. PREFECT PILATE'S PRAETORIUM OFFICE - EVENING

Pilate brings a chalice of wine over to the table and sets it down in front of Jesus.

PILATE: They say it's a good wine. I hope you like it.

Jesus smiles and reaches for the chalice for a taste.

CHRIST: Thank you.

Pilate sits across the table from Jesus, and sips from his own goblet. Pilate takes a big sigh.

PILATE: Tell me about the Baptist. Was he like you?

Jesus smiles.

CHRIST: There was no one like John the Baptist.

PILATE: I mean was he a sage like you?

CHRIST: He was a passionate spirit. I loved him very much.

Pilate winces.

PILATE: Herod said he was just a mad zealot.

CHRIST: John was a visionary.

PILATE: It appears he did not envision Antipas taking his head.

CHRIST: John understood his destiny.

PILATE: If it did not offend Tiberius, I should have had Herod's head on a platter long ago.

CHRIST: One violence for another, Pilate. Where does it end?

PILATE: Ask your God. He seems to routinely destroy his best messengers.

CHRIST: There is a larger view than our eyes can see. Some things are necessary.

PILATE: Destiny. That's what you like to say. Is it all as simple as that?

CHRIST: Why complicate it?

PILATE: The complication for me is the blood on my hands. I am not a lackey like Herod. I want no part in this.

CHRIST: Do you complain thus to Caesar regarding your appointed tasks?

Pilate does not respond.

CHRIST: You do not because it is your prescribed duty to govern Roman conquests. Yet how much more is it your duty to serve the Creator of man without question?

PILATE: So if I am to understand this correctly, I serve your God by killing his son?

Jesus smiles. He owes Pilate a little room here.

PILATE: The world is a strange enough place, but I must confess that I find your particular corner of it very peculiar my friend.

Pilate leans back and sighs.

PILATE: In fact, whenever I am around you, I am not sure that I know anything for certain.

Jesus chuckles at this and smiles tenderly.

CHRIST: Truly, what can we know more than a blade of grass? What can we do more than love?

Pilate smiles appreciatively at Jesus' simplicity.

PILATE: After all this has come to pass, I will hate myself for doing to you what you ask of me.

CHRIST: Of what use is it to curse a storm once it has passed? When the wind stops it carries with it no burden of what it has blown hither.

PILATE: Nevertheless, I am certain this contemptible deed will careen headlong into hell, dragging me with it.

CHRIST: Maybe, if you believe this act belongs to you.

PILATE: The death sentence will be my order. Who else would it belong to?

CHRIST: It belongs to no one, until it has come to pass. And then it belongs to the ages.

There is a moment as Pilate plumbs the depths of this comment.

CHRIST: This was also difficult for Iscariot to understand.

Pilate sobers up for a moment.

PILATE: Why do you mention this man?

Jesus does not respond, but Pilate feels transparent.

PILATE: You know that I spoke with him somehow.

Again Jesus does not respond. Pilate feels the need to confess.

PILATE: The soldiers at your arrest told me one of your disciples, Judas Iscariot, had led them to your group and pointed you out as the man to be arrested. It appeared that Judas had colluded with members of the Sanhedrin in the matter. I wanted to catch Caiaphas in a conspiracy, maybe nail him to the cross instead. So I had Iscariot brought to my chambers to speak with him about it.

CHRIST: And what did you discover in your conversation with Judas?

Pilate looks at Jesus directly for several moments.

PILATE: I discovered a man, like me, who is stricken with guilt over his relationship with you. And like me he struggles with this feeling that you are orchestrating something you want to have happen - you and your God. I felt pity for him, because I understood his struggle, and I could see that he loved you.

CHRIST: Judas is dear to me.

PILATE: Judas betrayed you.

CHRIST: Judas' struggle with his own meaning and purpose is a very powerful one, and in many ways represents a kind of courage uncommon to many who follow me.

PILATE: How is that?

CHRIST: He is not afraid to move outside of my influence to follow what matters to him.

Pilate is marveling at Jesus and shakes his head.

PILATE: How do you do it? You seem to be at peace with everyone, friend or foe. I would trade places with you if I

could, for such a sense of peace. Even with a death sentence
hanging over you.

CHRIST: Death has no jurisdiction over what lives truly.

PILATE: You speak like an Olympian god. Are you immortal?

CHRIST: Jesus is not immortal. But that which made him is.

Pilate raises his goblet in a mock toast.

PILATE: The gods live forever. Yet we are born to die.

CHRIST: How can this be? The Creator and the created are
not separate.

PILATE: And yet I am mortal. You are mortal. Our lives come
to an end. Is it not true?

CHRIST: Brother, where is the life in the Temple? Does it
exist in the columns, or the roof, or the arches? Or does it
live in the insight of the architect? For truly the temple will
be destroyed, but the dream of the builder shall not perish. Is
it not so here in Jerusalem where temple after temple is
destroyed? Yet the spirit of Solomon remains. And so it is
with the soul and the flesh. The body shall be born and pass,
but the spirit of the Creator which occupies it, shall not
cease to be.

*Pilate shakes his head. The notion of spirit is not satisfying him. He
gets up out of his chair.*

PILATE: So says the carpenter. I am a soldier. I have seen too
many men die. I'll tell you, there is nothing after death.

CHRIST: Tomorrow I return to nothing, where everything
awaits.

PILATE: How come I do not see what you see?

Jesus raises his chalice of wine.

CHRIST: A different kind of wine frustrates your sobriety and
your vision.

PILATE: (*smirking*) By what name is this wine known? I will have it destroyed immediately!

CHRIST: (*smiling softly*) It goes by the name Pontius Pilate.

INT. EMPTY STAGE - SPOTLIGHT ON ZARAH

ZARAH: I didn't want Jesus to die, though I knew it was his destiny. It is said that no creature in Jerusalem slept peacefully the night before Jesus' crucifixion. There was a sense, no matter if you hated or loved him, that something extraordinary was going to be taken from us. Pilate shared bread and wine with Jesus well into the night, talking with him as you would a dear friend. It was perhaps the Prefect's finest hour.

INT. PREFECT PILATE'S PRAETORIUM OFFICE - MORNING OF CRUCIFIXION.

The men have been up all night talking. Pilate, exhausted, sits across from Jesus, forehead in his hands.

PILATE: Do you know how many men I have sentenced to death?

Jesus does not respond.

PILATE: Crucifixion is ugly, I have never liked it. All politics. Rome likes the spectacle of it, the impact it has on the public. It disgusts me. I would rather choke a man to death with my bare hands than watch him humiliated in death on a cross. The only man worthy of crucifixion is the man who invented it.

Pilate addresses Jesus directly.

PILATE: They will have you hanging there, on display. They want to make an example out of you, Jesus of Nazareth. They will say, "He's no God, he's just a fool that bleeds like the rest of us." They will delight in watching you die slowly. Laugh, ridicule, and mock all your suffering. I know exactly what is awaiting you. A rat should not suffer such indignity in death.

CHRIST: The hour of deliverance is at hand, Pilate.

PILATE: Look how young you are. Why would any god find more value in your death than in your life?

CHRIST: This question was on my lips at Gethsemane Garden the night of my arrest.

PILATE: Did your God give you an answer?

CHRIST: I sought no answer. I wanted only to melt into the question.

PILATE: This God of yours is too mysterious for me.

CHRIST: My dear brother, mystery is a welcome condition for the truly faithful.

PILATE: I would rather have certainty.

CHRIST: The need for certainty is the birthplace of suffering.

Pilate drops his head and pulls at his hair.

PILATE: You speak to me in riddles, and with every one, I seem to know less and less.

CHRIST: And so the Sphinx, crouched in the desert, taunts the unsettled soul towards worlds unknown, and into the uncertainty of wild places; where we are compelled to vigilance, and not to slumber.

Pilate shakes his head.

PILATE: You must remain among us longer.

Jesus smiles warmly.

CHRIST: My destiny has never been about the endowment of extended years, Pilate.

PILATE: Forgive me for pressing you on the matter, but I

know that you are a great teacher, is it not so? Greater even than Socrates and Aristotle.

CHRIST: My ministry is to endure the dark night of the soul. That is all.

PILATE: What man can endure the horrors of this world without contraction? The task is too immense. I have seen enough to know that the cruelty of this life is not wholly reconcilable to any man.

CHRIST: I will realize in this world the victory of heart in the face of human error. I require this horrific affliction to descend upon me, so that I may overcome the abominations of men, as a testimony of what is possible in the flesh.

PILATE: There is heroic, and then there is impossible. These divine virtues you pursue, surely they are beyond the purview of the flesh. Are they not the sole domain of the gods?

CHRIST: I bear good news; the Creator withholds nothing from creation. We may on earth, inherit and occupy all that is possible in heaven. You yourself shall bare witness to this today.

Pilate weakly argues one last point.

PILATE: Are any of us really worth the price you must pay to deliver this good news?

Jesus puts his hand on Pilate's shoulder.

CHRIST: 'Worth' is a tragic notion.

Jesus looks up as if he has just heard something from the heavens. He looks back down at Pilate with a resolute gaze.

CHRIST: It is time now.

Pilate nods. His eyes begin to well up with tears as he summons the five execution centurions and the centurion captain from outside by hand gesture, who come in immediately.

PILATE: (*to the Centurion Captain*) Take him.

Jesus is escorted toward the door by the guards. Just before they reach it, Pilate speaks up.

PILATE: Jesus, I must tell you, Herod Antipas is here.

Jesus smiles.

CHRIST: Of course he is.

PILATE: How can you smile at this? He and his cronies wish to have access to you; to mock, humiliate and scourge you in preparation for your march to Golgotha. But he knows he is under my jurisdiction in this city, and that I will keep him away from you.

CHRIST: Let him play his hand.

PILATE: Why entertain this barbarian?

CHRIST: Herod believes he has power, but he has nothing but a villainous part in a play he did not author. He will act out his ghoulish role.

PILATE: Is the cross not enough?

CHRIST: Hear me when I say unto you, among the dark transgressions of mankind, love may be glorified most in its deepest violation. As my witness Pilate, let it be so today.

INT. EMPTY STAGE - SPOTLIGHT ON ZARAH

ZARAH: And so it came to pass that Herod Antipas had his sadistic way with Jesus; driving a crown of thorns into his head and draping a purple robe around him in mock majesty. Pilate's horror could not have been deeper, but this time he found a deep restraint and did not fail his friend Jesus; from his balcony watching the scourge, he remained present as a devoted witness without turning away, or lashing out in a rage against Antipas. In this moment he surpassed the devotion of many of Jesus' own disciples by remaining present in Jesus' final hours of suffering. But when Jesus left Pilate's sight on the way to

Golgotha, Pilate could not contain his woes, and he withdrew to his private chamber, inconsolable.

INT. PILATE'S BEDROOM CHAMBER

Pilate stares out the window, eyes glazed into the horizon.

PILATE: What troubled wind lashes at the door of my soul? Would that I could answer, and say to the brewing storm that stirs outside, "Come, enter." But I cannot. Nor can I shout from behind my domestic ramparts "Go away!" There is only a dread silence from within. The house is not empty, but the householder is. Where does he go when each room has become a self-decorated prison, with furnishings that lull me to sleep? I built this life called Pontius Pilate with my own hands, like a man who fashions his own crypt. I wanted these columns, this roof, and these walls to provide for me a grand shelter, but I found instead only a cold repository for the same stale air I have been breathing over and over my whole life. A man dies today on a cross of wood, and his death has more life in it than all my years of living will ever know. Jesus, the man who seeks no shelter, has found a way to be at home inside the very storms hollow men like me flee from. I condemned him to death in the very same hour that he offered me life. Now shall I let this new awakening in me die with the messenger. How is it that I find more occasion to say goodbye than hello in this world?

INT. EMPTY STAGE - SPOTLIGHT ON ZARAH:

ZARAH: I followed Jesus with the crowd, all the way to Golgotha. I was determined to be with him until he died. I wanted him to feel that I was there for him, like he had been for me. After too many hours of suffering, the centurion finally pierced his side, and as the fluids drained out of him, so too did the light left in his body. He groaned that it was "finished," and I felt his spirit expand out in every direction from his form on the cross. I waited for the empty feeling to grip me, the feeling of him ceasing to exist, but it never came. There was no ending. The flesh of Jesus had never been the life in Jesus.

Zarah turns her face toward the side of the stage as if she hears something from behind her.

ZARAH: Pilate, upon hearing of Jesus' passing, summoned me immediately.

INT. PILATE'S PRAETORIUM OFFICE - EVENING

Pilate looks out the window, lost in thought. Zarah enters the room behind him. He does not sense her presence there.

She stands for a moment just staring at him from behind.

ZARAH: Pilate.

Pilate turns around.

PILATE: *(somberly)* Is it finished?

ZARAH: Yes.

Pilate nods and slowly turns back to look out the window.

PILATE: Six hours of suffering on the cross at my order.

Pilate becomes briefly still, and after a moment he addresses her without turning around to face her.

PILATE: And you. How many years have you suffered under my orders, Zarah?

Zarah does not answer. After several moments Pilate continues, still staring off in the distance.

PILATE: You told me not to kill him. I didn't listen to you.

ZARAH: That was a young girl talking. A young girl who just wanted something for herself. You were stronger than me.

Pilate turns to face her.

ZARAH: Prefect, you were dear to him, because in the end, you did what he asked you to do.

Pilate begins to tear up. He turns and looks back out the window. After a few moments he speaks to her without turning around.

PILATE: I give you leave of this cursed arrangement. You will never again be troubled to attend to me. I will see to it your family is compensated somehow for the pain I have caused them.

Zarah, nods her head as tears now roll down her cheeks.

ZARAH: Pontius...

Without turning to face her, Pilate raises his hand and interrupts her.

PILATE: *(interrupting)* Just go, Zarah. Now, before my weaknesses return.

FADE TO BLACK

EPILOGUE

FADE IN SPOTLIGHT

INT. EMPTY STAGE - SPOTLIGHT ON ZARAH

Zarah is older now, clearly a woman. She is dressed in the clothing of common women of the day. She stands on the edge of the stage now looking out and speaking to the audience as if that theater were filled with her very own followers.

She is direct, clear, calm, poised and in her power.

ZARAH: Jesus as a man is hard to explain to anyone who had never met him personally. For those of us who had, our lives were never the same afterward. Pilate, true to his word never summoned me again. But like Icarus, it seems he had flown too close to a celestial light that became his undoing. The new window of humanness that Jesus had inspired in Pilate ultimately closed, and in time became sealed shut forever; just as Pilate himself had feared. And like Judas, Pilate too would eventually take his own life. As for myself, I can never forget those hours beneath Jesus as he suffered from his wounds on the cross. I recall how he would look down at us, amid the agony of crucifixion, with only kindness in his eyes. What kind of a man can do that? You can't explain it. But I will tell you that it washes every dark thing that has ever happened to you away forever. The night before they crucified him, in his prison cell, he made a frightened girl a promise. It was a promise that I know actually belongs to all of us. He told me that he would never really go away, and that he would always be with me, because in his kingdom, time had no bearing, and love had no boundary. Jesus changed my life, and he never broke his promise.

THE END

71

www.ingramcontent.com/pod-product-compliance
Lightning Source LLC
Chambersburg PA
CBHW021435110726
47901CB00008B/2431